SPOOK

by JANE LITTLE

Illustrated by SUZANNE KESTELOO LARSEN

SCHOLASTIC BOOK SERVICES
NEW YORK • TORONTO • LONDON • AUCKLAND • SYDNEY • TOKYO

Text copyright © 1965 by Jane Little. Illustrations copyright © 1965 by Suzanne
Larsen. This edition is published by Scholastic Book Services, a division of
Scholastic Magazines, Inc., by arrangement with Atheneum Publishers.

7th printing .... November 1974
Printed in the U.S.A.

To my family, with love.

Chapter 1

"COME ON, SPOOK," said the witch. "Wake up. We musn't be late for the meeting."

But the little black dog, curled up on the hearth, only huddled closer to himself.

"I'm not going," he growled, his eyes pressed tightly shut.

"Not going!" said the witch, whose name was Grimalda. "What kind of nonsense is that?"

She was sweeping her floor as she spoke, and since the dog would not move, she was obliged to make two neat piles on either side of him. Neat but nasty, for the dust of a witch's house is mixed with all manner of unspeakable things that fall from her worktable and kettle. These she gathered carefully into a large bottle marked "Spells — leftover," which she corked securely and set on a long shelf among hundreds of others containing magical ingredients.

This done, Grimalda turned again to the hearth.

"Get up, Spook," she said in a more threatening voice, and gave him a sharp poke with the handle of her broom.

Spook jumped to his feet with a faint yelp, and the witch shrieked in delight. Then she leaned her long yellow face down close to his.

"Don't you remember what night of all the year this is, sweetheart?" she demanded.

"My birthday?" faltered Spook in a low voice.

"Your birthday!" cried Grimalda. "Who cares about your birthday? It's Halloween, stupid. Halloween! Have you forgotten what business is afoot for us tonight? What miles we must travel? What mischief we must do before that silly rooster sets off his alarm and the fun is all over for another year?"

She spun around sharply on her heels and slapped a dish of cold bats' wings in front of the little dog. Then she sat down at her worktable to

a bubbling bowl of dark-green, soup, made from boiled young eels, shredded seaweed, and rotted turtles' eggs, for herself.

Spook sniffed at the leathery things in his dish.

"Why don't you keep a *cat*, like any other witch?" he whimpered. "What kind of life is this for a dog?"

"*You* know why," answered his mistress, dribbling soup off her pointed chin. "Because cats make me sneeze. That's why. Do you think I wouldn't rather fly to the meeting with an elegant black rascal of a cat on the handle than *you*, slipping and sliding and quaking all the way and likely to be airsick before we get there? Clumsy thing!"

"Why don't you go by yourself this time?" suggested Spook, reasonably.

"I can't go to the meeting without a familiar!" cried Grimalda, scandalized. "Every witch has to have a familiar. That's one of the first rules. And you're the only animal, so far, my antisneeze spell works on. Eat your food!"

Spook sighed very deeply and pushed away his untouched plate. He thought his nose felt rather hot. Could he be getting a fever? he wondered hopefully.

But Grimalda leaned down suddenly and snatched up his plate, which she hurled, together with her own, into an empty tub that stood by the hearth. Both dishes broke to pieces instantly upon landing in the tub.

"Wash!" commanded the witch. "And mend," she added, stamping her foot. A gurgle of soapy water began churning in the bottom of the tub, and the pieces of plate hastily scrambled about in it, trying to fit themselves back together.

As Grimalda readied herself for flight, Spook looked about the bare and blackened walls — just four of them — that were his home.

The witch had no use for more than one room, and everything in it was given over to the making and storing of spells. Over the wide-open throat of the hearth hung her great black kettle, smoldering ashes banked beneath it to keep the horrible things she brewed forever simmering there.

In Grimalda's house there was nothing whatever for comfort or pleasure. And the light was always dim, for a huge, jagged pine outside shadowed the one window by day, and by night the room was lighted only by the hearth and a single candle, burning on the witch's worktable. This table, with its chair, stood in the center of the room, its top stained red and blue and yellow and black like a bruise. On this, Grimalda ground and mixed her magic powders. Here she studied her moldering books of magic. Here she ate her meals, and here she slept with her head face downward under the high peaked hat she always wore.

Spook sighed again and wondered, as he had many times before, if there weren't some other kind of home for him, some other kind of voice than Grimalda's. The thought that there might be was like a secret promise, but since Grimalda never let him free, he had no way of finding out, and try as hard as he would, he could remember nothing before coming to live with the witch.

She planted both feet, in their buckled shoes, and the broom handle before him now.

"Climb on, Spook," she commanded. "Climb on, and we're away. We're away!"

At this, her voice rose to a piercing wail, and Spook mounted the broom handle with trembling paws.

"Away!" shrilled the witch again, and the broom handle upended with a sickening lurch, turned abruptly around, and shot through the window.

The wind skirled like bagpipes in his ears, and stars reeled in glittering streamers round Spook's head in the second before he clamped his eyes shut, clinging miserably to the broom handle with his short, blunt claws.

Chapter 2

In a distant cave, guarded by two sentinel crows and half hidden on a lonely hillside by thick brambles, the witches were gathering. Shrieking to one another and cackling with laughter, their ragged black draperies fluttering wildly about them, each witch circled the cave once and then swooped through the entrance to join her sisters. And on the handle of each witch's broom rode her familiar. Black cats, all of them, except one large green parrot, rusty and tattered with age, and Spook.

The heart of the cave lay deep in the hillside, and the passage that led to it was draped with bats hanging upside down in clusters like dark grapes. From its ceiling they peered down curiously at the witches darting along beneath them.

Grimalda snatched one or two as she went by, stuffing them hastily into her wide pockets, for what disagreeable purpose Spook knew only too well. He had no doubt they would be served to him for dinner next day.

It was in the cavernous heart of the cave that the witches came together. No light penetrated here at all, but each familiar was ordered to sit on a ledge above its mistress; together their eyes, magically aglow, made a ring of slanted green lights winking in the gloom. All except those of the parrot, who was blind with age.

As Grimalda glided in to take her place among the witches sitting in a circle round the walls of the cave, Spook squeezed against the hem of her skirt. Indeed, he would gladly have crept into her pocket, bats or no bats, as the terrible presence of almost a hundred cats hurtled at him like a charge of electricity. The hairs on his back stood upright, and he tried to throttle the growl that rose in his throat.

Grimalda settled herself on the floor and bared her scraggy teeth in a smile, first to the witch on her right and then to the one on her left. They both smiled hideously back. Spook hoped with every ounce of his small shaggy body that no notice would be taken of him. But suddenly Grimalda was hissing in his ear.

"Get to your ledge!" and she accompanied the command with a short jab of her bony forefinger.

Spook scrambled to the ledge, pressing himself close to the wall as the two cats who were his neighbors spat their displeasure.

In the center of the cave was a crude chair cut out of rock and carved with designs of animals and birds twisted about among strange letters and symbols. In this chair sat the Head Witch, bent forward with immense age, her straggly white hair hanging like fangs on either side of her head under its high peaked hat. She was very still, except for the glitter of her eyes and the occasional twitch of her long curved nose as she watched each witch enter and take her place. Digging his talons into her shoulder to keep his hold, sat the blind parrot. For he was *her* familiar.

As Head Witch, of course, she could do as she pleased, and since she greatly preferred birds to cats, she had long ago taken a parrot for herself.

When most of the rustling, hissing, mewing,

and cackling had died down, she spoke without rising, her voice like the slow grating of chains across a gravel path.

"Greetings to you, little sisters of the night. The sight of all your wicked faces is most welcome to me on this fearsome occasion."

Her eyes, piercingly sharp, rested for a moment on the ledge above Grimalda, and a slight frown darkened in them. But she went on:

"Once again we gather to celebrate Halloween. Once again we fly abroad to harry the land, to unsettle the night with mischief. And for each one of you, I have prepared a bag of tricks. But remember! The bags must be emptied — every trick in them used up — before midnight. My sentinels, who wait outside, will watch carefully and report to me if the night's work is not faithfully done. So make haste, little sisters, make haste! Collect your tricks!

> Some are merry,
> Some are sad,
> Some are cunning,
> *All* are bad.

Come get your tricks! Get your tricks!"

At her words, a great excitement bubbled

among the witches. They rose from their places, with a gabble of voices, and began swarming round the Head Witch, eager to accept the bulging black bags she was handing out.

"One at a time. One at a time," she shrilled, grinning with toothless delight until she came to Grimalda.

"Not so fast, dearie," she said, fastening her hands like claws onto Grimalda's arm. Pretending to be nearsighted, she squinted her eyes in Spook's direction.

"What is the meaning of that creature I see sitting on the ledge above your place? Do you call that a proper familiar to bring to the meeting?"

Grimalda, cowering, tried to answer. But the prickling in her nose could be held back no longer.

"Atchoo!" sneezed Grimalda. "Atchoo—atchoo!"

"What's that?" shrieked the Head Witch, and the old parrot, who had fallen into a doze on her shoulder, awoke with a squawk and bit her sharply on the ear. At this, she let loose her grip on Grimalda to reach round fiercely and yank at his tail feathers, most of which were already gone.

"Id's the catz," explained Grimalda stuffily. "They make me sneeze. Spells won't work on them. Only on *him*." She nodded resentfully at Spook.

"Nonsense!" screeched the Head Witch. "I

never heard of such a thing. If you haven't a proper familiar, you should be sent straight home to work on your spells instead of keeping Halloween with the rest of your sisters. However—" She glared for a moment in silence. "I shall overlook it this time. But see that you come with a proper familiar next Halloween, or don't come at all. Even if it takes you all year to discover a suitable spell."

She flung a lumpy black bag at Grimalda, who scurried off with it, pausing only to gather up Spook and her broom as she left.

Outside the cave, under the watchful eyes of the sentinel crows, Grimalda hastily adjusted Spook and the bag on the handle and rushed headlong into the air.

"Useless thing!" she muttered to Spook, who had clamped his eyes shut as soon as they took off.

Grimalda sneezed violently as she spoke, so that the broom, traveling at top speed, swayed dangerously. She sneezed once more and clutched at her teetering bag of tricks with one hand. With the other she reached for Spook. But her fingers closed on empty air. For below her, Spook was falling, round and round and down and down, his eyes shut, his paws waving helplessly as he went.

Chapter 3

Tumbling round and round as he fell, Spook's thoughts came in bursts, depending on when he was right side up.

Ever since he could remember, his dearest hope had been to get away from Grimalda. "But not to *fall* away," he thought in mounting panic, as he appeared to be gaining speed steadily with every turn.

Back in the cave, things had seemed as terrible as they could get for Spook, but now they were unquestionably getting worse. The chief question was what was he falling to or toward or into. On what would he land? Dare he open one eye just a crack? He dared.

The earth was zooming toward him, and just below he could see a circle of upturned faces around what looked like a giant cup of tea. There was a shout of, "Watch out, Jamie!" as Spook plunged into a cold shock of water that roared once and closed over his head.

Thrashing his way desperately to the surface, Spook found he was not alone. Someone else was thrashing with him and around and against him. As he broke through the surface, gulping frantically for air, he was seized by the scruff of the neck, hauled clear of the water, and dumped upon dry ground. Someone else was also dumped beside him.

Spook struggled to his feet, shaking a vigorous spray of water drops from his coat, and looked dazedly about him. In the fitful moonlight he could just make out the large loom of a house and the shadowy outline of a yard. He was surrounded by three persons, dressed all too familiarly for Spook's comfort.

The tallest, though not so tall as Grimalda, wore a fluttering black cape and a high peaked hat. Another, standing next to her, with a cutlass thrust into his belt, a skull and crossbones emblazoned on his tricornered hat, was unmistakably a pirate.

Beside the pirate, and smaller than he, was what seemed in the uncertain light to be a skeleton; and beside him on the grass, wet and shivering as himself but clutching an apple in one hand, was a small red devil.

Spook drew a shuddering sigh. There seemed to be no limit to how much worse things were going to get.

Then, crowding round the small red devil, they all began to speak at once:

"He's still holding his apple!"

"He's too young to duck for apples. I knew he would fall in. He's too young to go out with us at all."

"It wasn't his fault. The dog fell on him."

"Where did it fall *from*?"

They all turned to look at Spook, who dropped his tail between his legs.

"I wonder if he's friendly," the witch said.

"Friendly," thought Spook experimentally. He sniffed at the hand the witch offered him. "I wonder if I'm friendly. Yes, I'm sure I am." He tried licking the hand a little.

"Well, whether it was his fault or not, we'll have to take him back now," pronounced the pirate in tones of authority.

At this, the small red devil on the grass began
to sob.

"Don't cry, Jamie," said the witch in a kindly
way, and the skeleton leaned over to pat his wet
shoulder.

"There'll be another Halloween next year, you
know," said the skeleton. But Jamie's sobs rose to

such a howl of despair, Spook was tempted to join in.

Suddenly the kitchen door swung open, sending a yellow shaft of light to the figures around the rain barrel.

"Children, what on earth —" exclaimed their mother, standing there. Her voice carried a steady warmth that reached all the way out to Spook, so that he paused in his hasty effort to get as many legs between himself and the light as he could.

"Children," thought Spook, who had never seen any. "That's what they are. They're children."

"Why, Jamie's all wet," their mother went on. "Did he fall into the rain barrel? Bring him inside. Quickly."

The skeleton pulled Jamie to his feet, and they all began propelling him toward the open door. But at the entrance he broke away and hurried back to the rain barrel, where Spook still crouched under its shadow.

The boy reached down and scooped him up into his arms.

"He's wet too," said Jamie, carrying him, short legs bumping against Jamie's knees, into the kitchen with the others.

It was a big square kitchen with old-fashioned

cupboards and a rocking chair by a stove, from which the fragrance of gingerbread was sending a cheerful message.

Spook blinked in light brighter than he was accustomed to. As Jamie set him down, a huge golden-furred creature rose majestically from under the kitchen table and paced slowly toward him.

Spook's heart swelled and quivered inside his chest. He could hardly believe his nose, for it told him that this glorious animal was a dog. Another dog. Spook squirmed and sank to the floor as the great head touched his and he felt his ears delicately snuffed. Then he looked up into the golden eyes waiting above him, and the eyes smiled and the plumed tail waved grandly back and forth.

"See! Bounce likes him. He likes the little dog!" shrieked Jamie as his mother stripped off the devil suit and rubbed him with a towel.

Someone snatched Spook up in a towel too, and rubbed him so energetically he had a fleeting return of panic. It was the witch, whose name was Evelina. But she murmured softly to him while she rubbed, so that he grew calm at once. He grew calmer still when she placed him before a saucer of warm milk, and its warmth was transferred inside him.

Jamie was bundled into his pajamas, bathrobe, and slippers; and the four children sat down to applesauce and milk and thick brown chunks of the hot gingerbread their mother had just taken from the oven.

The great golden retriever resettled himself under the table as Spook licked up the last of the milk. He thought it more delicious than anything he'd ever imagined.

"I'll bet he was hungry," said Evelina. "I'll bet he hasn't eaten all day."

"I wonder whom he belongs to," said her brother John, wearing the pirate suit. "I've never seen him anywhere around here before."

"Where did he fall *from*?" asked Susan, the skeleton, not for the first time.

"I can tell you that," answered Spook eagerly. "I belong to a witch named Grimalda, and I fell from her broom into your rain barrel."

But no one paid the slightest attention to him. It was as if he had not spoken at all. They went on munching gingerbread and glancing from time to time, in a thoughtful way, at their mother.

It was John who, having swallowed down the last of his gingerbread, looked around the table and addressed his mother in a forthright, responsible manner.

"Look, Mother," he said. "Why can't we keep him?"

"Oh, John, we can't."

"Yes, Mother, please, please!" the others chorused.

"But we can't. We already have Bounce, and he's quite enough dog for one family."

"Please, Mother, please!"

Jamie tore away from the table, dropped dramatically on his knees, and threw his arms around Spook's neck.

"He fell on me. He's mine," claimed Jamie.

"But, children, he must belong to someone. You can't just keep someone's dog."

"He hasn't a collar," pointed out Susan. "Maybe he fell out of an airplane. He had to fall out of *something*."

All this while Spook's heart was traveling up and down like an elevator. He kept begging, "Please, please!" with the children, and they said, "Listen, he's crying."

"All right," said their mother at last. "We'll keep him overnight and call the pound in the morning. Then, if nobody claims him, he can stay. And *if* Father has no objection."

All four sprang up to congratulate her on this

wise decision, and Spook felt a strange thing begin to happen at the opposite end of him. He turned around to see what it could be, and discovered to his surprise that his tail was wagging. It had never wagged before, but once started, slowly at first and then faster and faster, it seemed it would never stop. He looked back hastily to see if he were doing something foolish, but an answering thump from under the table reassured him.

A telephone began to ring in another room as the three older children gathered up their masks and orange bags with **TRICK OR TREAT** written on them in black letters. Spook watched them go to the door, and then he turned to look at Jamie, whose face had settled into a threatening scowl.

"You stay home and take care of the little dog, dear," his mother said. She shut the kitchen door on Evelina, John, and Susan, and went off to answer the telephone, Bounce padding solemnly after her.

Jamie sat on for a time beside his empty plate with Spook curled at his feet. It was very quiet in the kitchen except for the ticking of the clock. Outside the kitchen window, the branch of an alder tree dipped in a sudden wind and brushed against the pane. The big red harvest moon was climbing higher, and a long black shadow passed across it and back again and then dipped swiftly downward.

Jamie slipped from his chair and pulled the cord of his bathrobe tight around him. He picked up his devil's mask from the chair where it hung and fastened it across his eyes.

"Come on, little dog," he whispered and tiptoed to the door.

Spook hastened to his feet and trotted after him. Very softly Jamie opened the door and dropped out into the night. Spook followed.

Behind them the quiet house seemed to wait in the shadows. Five minutes later a long yellow face under a high peaked hat peered cautiously through a window into the brightly lit kitchen. But of course it was now quite empty.

Chapter 4

GRIMALDA, for it was she, scrambled down from the black bag of tricks upon which she had been standing to get a good view into the kitchen. For a baffled moment or two, her eyes darted in every direction about the yard. Had the scent grown cold? Falling to her knees, she laid her long bumpy nose to the ground, where it twitched this way and that.

A witch's nose is one of her most useful powers. It is as keen as a bloodhound's when not disturbed by sneezing, and by this time Grimalda's no longer was. It soon brought her the answer she sought.

With a triumphant "Ha!" she sprang to her feet and set off on her way. This time, however, she thrust the broom handle through her bag of tricks and carried it on her shoulder like a knapsack. Travel by broom would never do where Grimalda wished to go.

She glided across the moonlit yard and let herself soundlessly through the gate that opened onto the street. There she started off without any further hesitation.

The street along which Grimalda moved was blotted out in darkness, except where an occasional street lamp threw down its pool of light and where lights from the houses twinkled like birthday candles up and down either side. It smelled of autumn leaves and mist, and a feeling of excitement stirred in the air.

Farther along the same street, Spook trotted close at Jamie's heels. He had no idea where Jamie would take him, and he didn't care. He could feel a powerful urge to follow wherever Jamie might go, and it seemed to Spook that he had found at last what he had been meant for all along. This thought made him so comfortable he simply couldn't bother to think about anything else.

Now and then he noticed small bands of hobgoblins, ghosts, and devils flitting by or gathering in knots to knock at someone's door and then come streaming back into the street, laughing and stuffing candy into the "Trick or Treat" bags they carried. But of Grimalda's presence several blocks behind him he was unaware.

"In a little while," Jamie told Spook, "we will catch up with Evelina and the others, because I know which way they were going. And by *that* time we should be so far from home they won't be able to take me back until they've finished."

Spook admired Jamie's plan and told him so. But Jamie mistook his meaning.

"If you're making that noise because you're hungry," he said, "I'm sure they'll share their treats with us when we find them." He reached down to pat Spook's head.

Spook found this answer so puzzling, he felt he must explain his remark to Jamie.

"I'm not hungry just now," he began politely. "I only wanted to say —"

But Jamie laid a warning finger to his lips.

"Hush," he said.

The measured sound of heavy footfalls approaching brought Jamie and Spook to a halt in the shadow of a huge rhododendron bush. In a moment, a ponderous blue-coated figure appeared under the next street lamp, swinging a short stick and humming briskly to himself.

When he saw who it was, Jamie pushed the devil's mask up on his forehead. "Hello, Mr. Brugle," he called.

But Mr. Brugle didn't have time to answer. For, speeding toward him like a black cloud, from the opposite direction, came a tall figure. It was Grimalda.

For one horrified second Spook's feet froze to

the ground, every hair on his back rising like the bristles on a brush. Then he dove straight between Jamie's legs and into the rhododendron bush, sprawling Jamie to the sidewalk. And Grimalda — head down, nose to the wind — ran directly into Mr. Brugle, her broom handle colliding painfully with his burly chest.

"Here, here," grunted Mr. Brugle, untangling himself from Grimalda and her broom. "What's the hurry? Where's the fire?"

"Fire?" shrieked the witch, whirling around to see if there was one behind her. As she did so, the sweeping end of the broom grazed Mr. Brugle's chin.

"Here, here," said Mr. Brugle again. "You'd better let me take that. You're liable to hurt somebody with it. What do you want with a broom anyway?" And he took a firm hold upon Grimalda's most prized possession.

"No!" she screamed. "No! No! No!"

At each "No!" she jumped off the ground with both feet, tugging at the other end of the broom.

From the shelter of his bush Spook watched Jamie roll out of the way and get to his feet. Mr. Brugle and Grimalda reeled about the sidewalk, while the broom seemed to hover on its

own between them. Spook was not surprised to see
that Mr. Brugle, puffing and blowing from exertion,
was the first to give in.

"All right," he said. "No need to take on so.
The broom goes with your witch's outfit, I suppose.
But aren't you a little big to be out trick-or-
treating?"

"I'm looking for my dog," Grimalda said sulkily. "He's gotten away."

"Say, that's too bad." Mr. Brugle drew a small black book from his breast pocket. "What does he look like?"

"Like a mistake somebody made." Grimalda grimaced self-consciously and looked down at her broom. "He's short and black and bristly."

Jamie started at this and backed protectively toward the rhododendron bush.

"Has he been missing long?" Mr. Brugle inquired.

"Not very," answered Grimalda. "He's just around here somewhere." She smacked her lips. "And when I find him, he's going right into this bag!"

She began to turn, first in one direction and then another, casting about, Spook knew, to catch his scent. But on the street where Jamie lived there were a dozen dogs or more. In no time she picked up the track of one of them, and without another word raced off in the darkness.

"Well," said Mr. Brugle, gazing after her. "That's an odd one. I don't ever recall seeing *her* before. She must belong to that new family in the yellow house. Moved in last week. Well!"

He turned around to study Jamie. "And now, sir, how about you? Pretty late to be out alone, isn't it?" His eyes traveled slowly from Jamie's red-masked head to his bedroom-slippered feet. "You look as if you were about ready for bed."

"I'm just catching up with Evelina and the others, Mr. Brugle," Jamie said, casting an anxious glance back of him. "I — I was delayed."

"H'm. Well, supposing I come along and help you catch up with them." The policeman placed a fatherly hand on Jamie's shoulder.

"Now which way did you say they went?" he asked.

From the rhododendron bush, Spook watched miserably as Jamie took a step forward. The little boy hesitated a moment and then, as though he had no choice, started off with Mr. Brugle.

He didn't go far, however. Just as Spook was wondering if he should follow after them, he heard Jamie say, "Look, Mr. Brugle. I dropped something. There by the big bush. I'll have to go and get it."

Jamie broke away from the policeman and hurried back to the bush. Leaning down, he whispered, "You stay here, little dog. Don't go away. I'll come for you later."

"I want to come with you, Jamie," Spook answered. "I'm not afraid."

But Jamie misunderstood him again. "Good boy," he said, patting Spook's head. Then he was off again with Mr. Brugle, down the street where Grimalda had gone.

Before they quite disappeared from sight, Spook crept from his hiding place. Keeping to the shadow, his tail drooping dejectedly, he proceeded on small determined feet as rapidly as possible after Jamie.

Chapter 5

Spook jogged along alone for a block or two until, rounding a sudden curve in the street, he came upon a party somewhat larger than he had expected. He thought it sensible, therefore, to stop behind a garbage can.

Mr. Brugle, one large hand still on Jamie's shoulder, was standing in the midst of the group. Spook easily picked out Evelina, John, and Susan, who appeared to have been joined by a number of friends, all dressed for Halloween.

"It's all right, Mr. Brugle," Evelina was saying sweetly. "We'll take care of him now and see that he gets safely home."

But the look she bent on her small brother, standing forlornly before her in his night clothes, was a stern one.

"That's right, Mr. Brugle. We'll be responsible for him," John said impressively.

Everyone waited in silence as Mr. Brugle delivered Jamie into the custody of his family and, in further silence, until the policeman, satisfied that all was well with his charge, continued on his beat.

Then:

"I *told* you. He's too young for Halloween."

"Now someone will have to take him home."

"Does Mother know he followed us?"

"Oh, let him stay."

"We might as well, I guess."

Jamie stood with respectfully lowered head while his fate was being decided by his elders. Once a favorable decision was reached, however, he took a long, careful look down the shadowy street before settling his devil's mask again on his face.

"He's wondering where I am," thought Spook. "I'll creep up behind him, and he won't know I'm there until I push my nose into his hand. Then there I'll be!"

Very intent on this plan, he drew cautiously nearer the crowd of children now fanning up the broad stoop of a large white house. Someone rang the bell, and someone giggled. Spook placed one foot and then another on the bottom step.

The door at the top of the stoop was flung open by a tall lady.

"Trick or treat," chorused the children.

"Trick or treat," hissed a voice in his ear.

Spook tore his eyes away from the figure of Jamie he had been keeping in view and stared straight into Grimalda's gloating face.

"On your way to a party, love?" she purred. One hand stole like a claw from her side.

Spook gathered all the strength he could summon into his short, sturdy hindquarters. As Grimalda reached for him, he hurled himself toward the last pair of feet crowding across the lighted threshold above. And Grimalda sprang after him, her black cape aflutter about her heels.

A jack-o'-lantern stood in an orange glow just outside the door, grinning crookedly to himself. As Grimalda leaped by, the edge of her cape caught the twig in his cap and knocked it askew. The candle flame flared and licked out at the billowing black cloth.

"Mind your manners there, Jack," hooted Grimalda, pausing at the doorway. She dipped swiftly into the black bag on her back, and a little cloud passed over the jack-o'-lantern. When it was gone, the pumpkin was nowhere to be seen, but in its place was a large yellow onion, its face carved into a dismal frown, bitter tears oozing from its hollow eyes.

"Have a hanky?" Grimalda offered jovially, and she tossed a scrap of black material at the melancholy vegetable.

Spook took advantage of this interruption to hide himself among the children as they went into the house. Grimalda, following behind, caught up with him easily. But she made only a few half-hearted grabs in his direction, which he dodged, running between the children's legs. She was beginning to enjoy herself, he could see, and so was in no great hurry to retrieve him.

A table had been set up in the hallway, loaded with cider and cookies, a shining mound of red apples, a dish of candies wrapped in colored papers and another full of pennies in the center. Here everyone was collecting, and Grimalda, with a glower at Spook, hastened to join them.

Spook decided to postpone his reunion with Jamie, and as soon as the witch's back was turned, he slipped beneath a window curtain that hung to the floor.

Feeling safer, Spook watched Grimalda sidle up to the young person dressed most like herself.

"How did *you* get here?" she asked pleasantly.

Evelina stared at her for a moment.

"How did *you*?" replied Evelina coldly.

"Hee-hee. The same as you, I expect. I flew," cawed Grimalda, preparing to give her new friend a playful poke with the broom handle.

But the tall lady had gone from the hall for a moment, and Evelina's attention was diverted to the treats table.

"Jamie," she called over the heads of the jostling children. "Don't grab so."

Grimalda's shrill laughter split the air.

"Jamie," she called out, mocking Evelina. "Don't grab so. Grab *so*!"

She thrust her way to the table and, seizing a handful of doughnuts, flung them into the air, holding her exceedingly long, bony forefinger aloft like a spike to catch them neatly, one by one, as they came tumbling down. Then she swept the finger, ornamented with doughnuts, into her mouth, gobbled every one and brought it out again, licking off the last of the sugar.

Before anyone had recovered from this, she was twirling a plate of cookies high above her peaked hat, round and round.

"Have a cookie, Spook, old familiar. I know you're there, under the curtain. Come out and join the lovely party we're having."

She hurled the spinning plate over Spook's terrified head. It sailed through the window and landed with a clatter outside.

Some of the younger children set up a wail at this and a grownup, appearing suddenly in the doorway, called severely, "See here, young lady, this has gone far enough!"

"Where's *your* familiar, my dear?" Grimalda inquired of Evelina in a confidential tone.

"My *familiar*?" echoed Evelina.

"Yes, mine's been missing, and I've only just now discovered him. Beneath the window curtain by the door. My nose, you know. It seldom fails."

She turned away from Evelina and began a gleeful dance. Grimalda's feet, in their pointed shoes, shot up and down like pistons, her black skirts whirling in a tempest about her skinny legs.

She threw a shower of pennies into the air, and they came down, at her command, a cloud of coppery moths that flew after the cookies out of the window. In her hands the shining apples turned to red rubber balls. "Here, catch!" she cried and set them bouncing against the walls and about the table, overturning cups of cider and scattering candy to the floor.

This was too much for anyone to bear. The older children stormed at the dodging witch, trying to catch at her fluttering garments, while the younger ones drew back fearfully. Grownups began to descend in earnest.

"They will surely stop her now," thought Spook, a faint hope for his own future rising within him.

But Grimalda took no notice of the menacing advance of people. She only danced the harder, accompanying the thump of her feet with the ring of her high-pitched laughter.

Then abruptly she stopped dead in her tracks, a look of horror settling on her face. Spook craned his neck around the curtain to see what she was staring at. It was a large marmalade cat, strolling down the hall directly toward Grimalda.

"Get your familiar out of here," she screamed to Evelina, "or I shall have to leave. Get it out. It will spoil the party. Get it out!"

As Evelina only stared and the cat continued its slow approach, Grimalda began to sneeze. One thunderous sneeze followed after another, until Spook was sure she would blow herself to pieces. Instead, she swooped over to his hiding place right in the middle of a sneeze. Stooping down, she swept him from the floor and into the black bag that hung from her shoulder.

The door stood open, and in a moment she was gone, the sound of her last violent sneeze still vibrating in the air.

Chapter 6

Bumping uncomfortably about among the queer things inside Grimalda's stuffy black bag, Spook could hear her racing footsteps as she sped along the street. Was there a pattering of other footsteps as well? He could not be sure. There was a light thud as Grimalda mounted the broom — now in flying position — settled the bag on the handle in front of her, and shrilled her command, "Away!"

But the broom failed to take off with its customary smooth thrust into the air. Spook felt as if something heavy had caught onto one end. It wobbled uncertainly, but would not rise.

"What's this? Who's there?" shrieked Grimalda, thrashing about. "Get off at once."

"I won't," said another voice. (It was Jamie's.) "Not unless you give me that little black dog."

"Give you that little black dog, indeed!" cried Grimalda indignantly. "It's clear you have no notion of private property, whoever you are. Spook is my property. And so is this broom. Now, get *off*!"

Spook heard the sound of scuffling and a slapping noise as Grimalda went on screaming, "Get off!" and Jamie panted, "I won't."

"Stay on. Stay on," Spook barked excitedly. Then he stopped to listen again.

Grimalda was shouting, "You can't stay on this broom. You are some sort of human, aren't you? It's against all the rules." And to the broom, "Now away! Away!"

The broom struggled frantically to obey, and at last, lurching this way and that, it rose into the air. Spook and whatever the things were in Grimalda's bag rolled against each other like ship's cargo in a storm at sea. First he jostled against something hard and then something soft. Something scratched his nose and something rapped him sharply on the head.

"Ouch," growled Spook, scrambling to get his head up and his feet down.

"I wonder whether Jamie is on or off," he thought when he had righted himself. "Oh, *on* I hope."

Outside on the broom handle, Grimalda seemed to have grown calmer.

"If you won't get off," she was saying, "at least sit still, so as to steady this broom while I think what is to be done with you."

"Jamie is still on the broom," sighed Spook to himself.

He tried poking his nose a bit against the top of the bag. The wild commotion of their take-off must have loosened the cord that held it shut, for it gave quite easily at his touch, and in a moment the bag sagged wide open. Spook found something solid beneath him that he could brace himself on, and by giving a little wiggle, he was able to push his head cautiously outside just as they cleared the whispering branches of a hickory tree. They staggered higher into the sky, and Spook's nose quivered gratefully at the cool rush of autumny air that greeted him.

Grimalda sat in her customary sidesaddle position, hunched in thought. Behind her was Jamie, astraddle the broom straws, both hands thrust before him for balance, his eyes wide and watchful on Grimalda. Spook dared not signal to him in any way for fear of dislodging the boy's hold on the broom or attracting Grimalda's attention.

In a little while they were flying more evenly and, peering over the top of the bag, Spook could

see streets and houses following in twinkling ribbons below them, gradually giving way to woodland and meadow, veiled and quiet. In fact, so peaceful was their progress after the evening's excitement, he found himself almost enjoying a ride on the broomstick for once, especially since Jamie was riding the broomstick too.

"If only I knew what was to become of us when we land," he thought.

The moon was traveling very high above them when Spook's keen ears caught the sound, faint but clear, of a faraway cawing. He strained his eyes into the shadowy night, and before long two immense black crows appeared, passed them, wheeled at some distance, and headed back. They were the sentinel crows from the witches' cave. Were they coming to see if Grimalda had used up her tricks?

He glanced at the witch, but she took no notice. Instead, she straightened abruptly and plunged her hand into the black bag. Careful to keep his head clear of the top, Spook tucked in his tail and pulled his legs close to himself.

"I don't want *you,* stupid," Grimalda muttered as her searching fingers pinched one of Spook's ears. Presently, her hand closed over something else and withdrew it from the bag of tricks.

"Aha. You will do, little beauty," she crooned. "You and I will contrive some special misery to fit this tiresome boy — to make him wish he had never been so eager to travel with us."

In the palm of her upturned hand, Grimalda held a tiny red cap, a jaunty sliver of a feather stuck in its band.

"You are the Shrinking Cap, I believe," Grimalda said to it. "Now listen carefully to what I wish you to do. I will put you on the boy's head. Cling tightly. Don't let go of him. Very quickly he must shrink, dwindle, shrivel—smaller—smaller — smaller. Until he is a tiny thing no bigger than my fist. Just the right size to fit you. Hee-hee. Then I'll reach into my pocket and bring out a bottle of Fixit. Spray you both, and there you'll be! Fixed forever to the handle of my broom. An ornament anyone would envy."

She grinned triumphantly and waved the little cap at Jamie. "How about *that* for a Halloween trick?"

"Oh no," begged Jamie. "Please, cap, don't shrink me. Please don't."

"You keep out of this, boy," snapped Grimalda. "This cap must obey my command. Besides, it's time I began to use up my tricks."

Even as she spoke, however, the two black crows bore down upon her with beaks stretched wide, their hoarse cries ripping the air.

Grimalda flung up one arm to drive them off, sweeping the little red cap from its perch.

Spook peered again over the top of the bag to watch the cap as it tumbled away into the darkness below. What astonished creature might it happen to land upon, he wondered, and begin at once to obey Grimalda's command: "Cling tightly—don't let go. Shrink—smaller—smaller—" The little dog shivered and returned his attention to the witch and the scolding crows.

"Go away! Be off!" Grimalda screamed at them. "No, I won't come with you. I won't. I have further business I must attend to."

The harsh cawing of the crows reminded Spook strongly of the Head Witch herself.

"I *have* the familiar right here," Grimalda shrieked back to them. "I had to put him in the bag because he tried to get away. Yes, I *know* the boy is not allowed, but he is just getting off. He's here without permission, anyway. I *have* used some of the tricks. Well — so far, only two. But there's still plenty of time. Oh, go *away*!"

For some agitated moments she continued to fend off the circling birds, while Jamie and Spook ducked down to avoid their flapping wings.

Then, quite suddenly, Grimalda's arms dropped to her lap, she seemed to shrink a little herself, and in a moment the broom was proceeding peacefully once more, the two crows flying silently on either side.

"Where *to*?" thought Spook.

Chapter 7

As soon as he saw the desolate hillside, with its thick cover of wood and bramble, Spook knew they were approaching the witches' cave.

Escorted by the sentinel crows, the broom dipped downward and came to rest outside the entrance where a giant tripod stood, outlined in the clear moonlight. From it hung an enormous kettle, and over this the Head Witch hovered, stirring with a long ladle the loathsome mess that bubbled inside. She was preparing a tempting brew for the witches, returning from their Halloween sport. And, indeed, many of them were already gathered about her, cackling merrily. Their

black bags — empty of tricks — were piled neatly to one side.

At sight of their mistress, the crows set up a hubbub of cawing. One flopped onto Grimalda's shoulder, and the other perched on her hat. They lifted their wings and pointed accusing beaks at Grimalda, as they poured out the tale of her disobedience.

The Head Witch swung around to face them, slimy drops dribbling from the ladle in her hand.

"What's that? What's that?" she demanded sharply. "Don't both talk at once. I can't make out a word you are saying."

This time they took it more slowly, and the Head Witch waggled her ancient head in horror as she listened, her eyes darting fiercely to the witch on the broom.

"Grimalda, Grimalda," she intoned as the crows cawed on. "The moon in her zenith, and your bag of tricks still unused! Traveling without a familiar in sight!" She waved her dripping ladle at Jamie. "And carrying a human creature! Here is wickedness of the wrong sort altogether."

Her gravelly old voice shook with rage. "You have seriously offended me, Grimalda. You have offended all your sisters."

Grimalda dismounted from her broom and stood with drooping head before the Head Witch, her black bag still bulging full at her feet and Jamie looking fearfully from behind her. The other witches took several steps backward, staring at Grimalda in shocked disbelief. Their familiars spat at the half-hidden dog peering from the top of Grimalda's black bag and leaped into the shadows at the mouth of the cave.

The two crows, having delivered their message, fell into a merciful silence and flew into the bushes to preen their feathers, with evident satisfaction at a job well done.

Laying down her ladle, the Head Witch hobbled to a pile of curiously arranged rocks nearby. Very slowly she lowered herself to this seat, unsettling the aged parrot that rode her shoulder so that he squawked sourly into her ear. As soon as she was seated, the other witches fluttered around her. They arranged themselves in huddled black rows at her feet, their pointed faces turned upward, eagerly awaiting what might happen next. Then the Head Witch summoned Grimalda with an imperious crook of her finger.

Grimalda obeyed, leaving behind her broom and the bag of tricks with Spook inside and Jamie standing uncertainly between them. Spook hoped the boy would not try to bolt for it into the wooded hillside. The dog longed to poke his head out further so that he could lick Jamie's hand, but he dared not.

"Well, Grimalda," the Head Witch began. "How do you account for yourself? How much mischief have you done tonight? A lot?"

Grimalda lowered her head again but made no answer.

"Some?" demanded the Head Witch.

Grimalda's face began to twitch, but she was still.

"Any at all?"

"Atchoo!" exploded Grimalda. "Atchoo! Atchoo!"

"What kind of an answer is that?" thundered the Head Witch.

"I had to sneeze," explained Grimalda. "Id's the catz."

"*Had* to sneeze? *Had* to sneeze? No witch *has* to sneeze. You must *control* yourself." She glanced over her shoulder at the cats crouching in the entrance of the cave. "Send those familiars deeper into the cave."

One of the witches scurried to do her bidding.

"Now, what were we about?" she went on to

Grimalda. "Ah yes. What mischief have you done?
Which of my tricks have you used? Fetch that
bag here!"

Her commanding finger shot out again, pointing
to the bag of tricks, and another witch sprang to
her feet. Spook ducked his head just as the bag
was whisked across the ground and dumped before
the Head Witch.

"Well," she roared. "Which of them have you used?"

"Only the Dark Cloud, at a party I attended, and the Shrinking Cap, on that boy, there," sniffed Grimalda in a low voice.

The Head Witch looked carefully at Jamie. "You lie!" she shrieked. "I don't know what you did at the party, but the boy has not been shrunk. He looks the usual size to me. Come here, boy."

Jamie advanced hesitatingly over the rough ground toward the ancient lady, his hands clenched at his sides. He had long since lost his mask and slippers, and the cord to his bathrobe had come undone.

"Now then, boy," said the Head Witch when he stopped just before her. "Tell me. How dared you take flight on the handle of a witch's broom?"

Jamie drew a quick breath and looked straight into her piercing eyes. "Because of the little dog," he said. "She stole the little dog and took him away in that black bag. I had to get him back."

"I didn't steal him," retorted Grimalda. "Spook is my property, and I can do with him what I like."

"*I* can do with him what *I* like, whatever and

whose ever he is," the Head Witch advised her nastily.

Grimalda fell silent at this, staring at her pointed toes. The Head Witch grinned in a satisfied way and waved her hand. "Shake out the bag, so that we may see what is left in it."

Two witches seized Grimalda's bag, turned it upside down, and shook. Spook, who was on top, rolled over twice and tumbled out. Scrambling up, he looked anxiously about him — at the ring of watchful witches and the Head Witch herself — at Grimalda, sullen and brooding — and at the little boy, standing forlornly in his bathrobe. Spook shook his coat once to gather his wits and then hurled himself straight at Jamie's feet.

The Head Witch flung her arms into the air. "It's the improper familiar!" she screamed. At this sudden movement, the outraged parrot bit her on the elbow. With a yelp of pain she snatched off her peaked hat, plucked the bird from her shoulder, loosening a shower of green feathers, and stuffed him into the crown. Then she replaced the hat on her head, and he was heard from no more.

After this interruption the witches went back

to shaking Grimalda's bag. An odd assortment of objects collected in a tangled mess on the ground — a skeleton, a shadow, a slim green snake, a small ghost, a rusty chain, a beaded pocketbook, and a lady's hat that looked like a beehive. The tricks were helplessly tangled and, to Spook's astonishment, they seemed to come alive as they poured from the bag. They did a great deal of kicking and calling of sharp names as they struggled to sort themselves out. The skeleton boxed briefly with the shadow, and the pocketbook snapped nervously at the snake's tail. But at last they came smartly to attention before the Head Witch.

She leaned forward to count them. "Seven," she said after counting twice. "Seven left over." A murmur of disapproval rippled through the witches seated about her, and the tricks looked quite shamefaced.

"Put yourselves away in the cave," said the Head Witch in not unkindly tones. "You will have to wait until next Halloween to be used. Well — it can't be helped."

The tricks turned in a trim row and marched into the cave, the snake hissing fussily and the chain rattling sharply to keep them in line.

The Head Witch watched them go and then

turned to Spook, still huddled close to Jamie and wishing he were invisible.

"Leave that boy at once, miserable animal, and go to your mistress. Unsuitable though you may be, she must make shift with you until she manages something better."

Spook took a desperate grip on his ebbing courage and approached the Head Witch.

"Please, Your Evilness," he tried in a trembling voice. "I'd rather stay with the boy."

"Nonsense," snorted the Head Witch. "You'd much better not. The boy is human, you know."

She paused, but when Spook could think of no answer to this, she went on in a solemn voice.

"You will discover, when you know them better, that humans have no regard for animals. Never allow them the slightest bit of fun. No turning into a bat or a bear or a butterfly. Once a dog always a dog is the kind of treatment you get from them."

Spook shivered. "I don't care," he said. "I'm comfortable just being a dog."

"And what about somebody to talk to?" the Head Witch continued. "They'll never understand a word you say. They could if they wanted to take the trouble, but they won't even try."

"I've noticed that," said Spook. "But I don't mind. I haven't so very much to say anyway, really."

"Whether you mind or not is of no importance," she said. "The point is, Grimalda cannot do without a familiar and *you*, however unsuitable, are *hers*."

Spook had a sudden, sad vision of Grimalda's house and himself curled up forever on her blackened hearth, a bowl of bats' wings in front of his nose. He dropped his head and crept stubbornly back to Jamie's bare feet.

Grimalda jerked up her head with a snort of impatience. She lunged toward Spook and made a quick pass with her hands over his head, mumbling a strange jumble of words.

At once, Spook began to feel very unlike himself. He seemed to be shrinking and rolling up like a sausage. The ground appeared to be closer than usual. Everything on it looked very large, and he wondered what had become of his feet. In a moment he was crawling on Jamie's foot in the fuzzy coat of a black and yellow caterpillar. Indeed, he had hardly realized he *was*

a caterpillar when he felt himself being scooped up in Jamie's hand and plunged into the pocket of his bathrobe.

But Spook barely had time to make out where he was before he was feeling queer again and bigger. The pocket began to swell and bulge and finally to rip. Then it came apart in all its seams and Spook fell to the ground. He was a small dog once more, and his head was a whirl of confusion. Jamie knelt down beside Spook and patted him all over to make sure he was really safe.

The Head Witch rocked with pleasure on her stony seat.

"Well done, boy," she chortled. "Oh, well done! You have outtricked Grimalda. You turned the familiar back to a dog."

Jamie looked up surprised. "*I* did?" he said.

"No doubt about it. Hee-hee. What a delight! But wait —"

Abruptly sober, her eyes glittered suspiciously at Jamie.

"How did you do it, eh? Could it be that you are — Are *you* a magician?" she demanded.

Chapter 8

"I — I DON'T THINK SO," faltered Jamie. "It's just that the little dog disappeared, and there was a caterpillar instead. I knew the caterpillar must really be Spook, so I picked him up to keep him from Grimalda, and as soon as I touched him, he was the little dog again. As soon as I touched him, he seemed to change."

The Head Witch received this explanation in silence, her gaze shuttling thoughtfully from Jamie to Grimalda.

"H'm," she said at length. "As soon as you

touched him, eh? Your power lies in your touch, then." She leered disagreeably at Grimalda. "The touch of love is what he possesses, my girl. This puts another light on the matter."

She heaved herself up in a flutter of black draperies and took a few tottering steps back and forth.

"The problem we have now is, how to deal with the boy. If he were an ordinary boy, it would be customary to dump him into the brew. Not directly, of course. First he should be softened by simmering in glue for an hour or so."

Her long nose twitched at the fumes from the bubbling kettle, and she smacked her lips with pleasure before going on.

"If, on the other hand, he *is* a magician and can match Grimalda's powers, he might make some claim to this familiar after all." She pushed thoughtfully at her lips with a bony forefinger. "And I should hardly like to simmer a magician even for an hour."

The other witches had been listening to her in breathless attention, and one of them spoke out shrilly:

"What about a contest, Ma'am? Can't we have a contest to see who shall have the familiar?"

"That's it!" shrieked the Head Witch. "A contest! What a splendid idea. This boy — or magician — against Grimalda." She sat down abruptly on the pile of rocks. "I'll be the judge. I'll make up the rules. Fair means or foul — both are equally good. And the familiar will be awarded to the winner."

"Does that mean," asked Jamie boldly, "that if I win I can keep him?"

"Right," beamed the Head Witch.

"But how do I get him home with me?" Jamie persisted.

"Transportation provided," boomed the Head Witch handsomely.

"And if I lose?" Jamie asked in a low voice.

"Then it's off with Grimalda that the familiar must go, and it's into the brew with you. Now don't interrupt. We must see to the scoring."

She beckoned to one of the crows, who flew cawing to her feet. Leaning over, the Head Witch drew two circles in the loose dirt with her fingers, one before Grimalda and one in front of Jamie.

"Whenever either side scores, drop a stone into the circle belonging to it," she told the crow, indicating with a sweep of her hand the pebbles that lay scattered near her pile of rocks.

The crow nodded and began pacing solemnly back and forth between the two circles, ready to carry out its duties.

"Now then," said the Head Witch. "Grimalda must use her powers upon the familiar, and the boy (or magician) must try to prevent her with his. The first side to score two times out of three is the winner. You may begin."

Grimalda stood very still for a moment, staring with narrowed eyes at Jamie and Spook. Then she brought her hands up and together, and made a lightning thrust at Spook.

At once he began to have the feeling that he was no longer himself. His body seemed to be dividing itself into two parts, with a hard covering, like a shell, encasing it. In addition to his own four legs, four more shot out of his sides, and they all began to grow long and pencil-thin, and to be covered with little pads of hair. He squinted as he waved one of them in front of him, trying to make out what kind of creature he had become. For although he now found he had eight eyes, none of them saw very well.

"Am I a crab?" he wondered. "Or a bug? Or maybe a spider? That's what I am. A spider."

He tried to see Jamie's face, but at first he

was too shortsighted and then, to his horror, he commenced to grow. Larger and larger and taller and taller on his long hairy legs. He shot past Jamie's frightened face and went on growing until the row of gaping witches looked like dolls below him. When he stopped at last, he was an enormous spider on eight gigantic legs, with two fangs curved like buffalo horns and eight eyes as big as soup plates.

Peering down, he discovered the tiny figure of Jamie backing frantically away from him. "Oh no, no," he begged silently, for he had no voice. "What shall I do? Oh, what *can* I do?"

Jamie was backing away from the row of witches toward the woodland when Spook, remembering he was a spider, began desperately to spin. Working his spinnerets as fast as he could, he sent a long, shimmering streamer of silk after Jamie, who had broken into a run now and was stumbling in his haste to take cover in the woods. The streamer caught him deftly about the waist and held him gently where he was.

Then, very slowly and very carefully, Spook closed the joints of his giant legs and folded them beneath him so that he was flat on the ground in front of the little boy. He bowed his terrible

head so that Jamie no longer could see it. "Don't be afraid. Oh, don't be afraid," he implored in his heart.

As he waited, not daring to look, he felt Jamie move against the silken tether. He heard one footstep and then another shuffle toward him. Another dreadful pause, and very slightly, just barely, he felt the tips of Jamie's fingers tap his horny back.

"Spook?" Jamie's voice quavered. "Spook?"

Before he could draw his breath in relief, Spook was restored to his own size and shape by Jamie's touch.

Jamie stared at Spook, and then his face broke into a big grin. "Come on," he said, and they raced back to the waiting witches.

"The boy has scored. Give the boy a stone!" the Head Witch called.

The crow bustled up with a stone in its beak. As it passed Grimalda, she stuck out her foot and neatly tripped the big black bird, popping the stone from its beak. With a furious squawk at Grimalda, it recovered the stone and finished its errand on the wing.

Grimalda scowled and brought up her hands to make another gesture at Spook. He felt himself changing again. Shrinking this time, shriveling, melting. He was very warm and growing warmer. Warmer and smaller, much smaller. Heat spread all through him, until he glowed and pulsed with it and he thought it must be eating him up.

"What can I be?" he thought. "Whatever I am, if Jamie touches me I will surely burn him."

He could hear the witches catch their breath in a long "A—a—ah" as Jamie put out his hand.

"Clever Grimalda! Cunning Grimalda!" they chanted. "She's changed the familiar into a live coal — a live coal!"

Jamie's hand reached out — nearer and nearer — but then he drew it hastily back. The witches let out their breath in a hiss of triumph.

Again, slowly, the boy held out his hand while Spook tried to withold his heat, to bank his fire. But again Jamie's hand fell back, and again the witches hissed their triumph.

Jamie pulled the cord of his bathrobe tight around him and tried for the third time to touch the glowing coal. He stretched his arm out its full length. The tips of his fingers turned scarlet from its nearness, but in the end he drew back his hand as before, and the witches jeered gleefully.

Then the Head Witch called, "A stone for

Grimalda. Give Grimalda a stone. Her power has prevailed. Proceed."

Grimalda was ready for him with a wave of her hands, and Spook was changing again. His fire was cooling. He felt himself growing lighter, thinner, as though something were smoothing him out and pressing him into flatness. He felt frail and rather brittle. "What am I now?" he wondered. "A piece of paper? No. I am more than that. A leaf."

He lay upon the ground waiting for Jamie to pick him up. "Hurry," he whispered. "Hurry."

Grimalda was standing with her neck stretched out, her hands planted on her hips. She blew such a blast of air, it tumbled her hat forward on her face and sent Spook whirling dizzily over Jamie's head. Jamie snatched at him, but he skimmed just above the boy's frantic reach. Then he drifted gently off toward the Head Witch and down, down right into the black folds of her lap.

There was a chorus of cackling laughter from the witches and then silence, as they watched to see what Jamie would do. Jamie ducked his head and gulped as he gazed at the terrible old lady above him. She sat perfectly still in the calm moonlight, the autumn leaf on her lap.

Slowly Jamie edged near. When he was close enough to reach the leaf with his finger tips, his hand came out from behind his back and he stole toward Spook. "Hurry, hurry," Spook urged him silently.

Then Grimalda shoved her hat back on her forehead and blew another giant blast at Spook. He fluttered into the air, sailed again over Jamie's head, just out of reach, and came to rest in a whole pile of leaves that had drifted against the rocks. All about him he could hear them rustling and whispering dryly to one another. Hundreds of them, he was sure. How would Jamie ever know which was the right one?

Jamie, who had followed the flight of the leaf with his eyes, stood over the pile into which Spook had disappeared, a perplexed frown on his face. "If he tries to guess which leaf I am and misses, they won't give him another chance. Grimalda won the last point after he had three tries. This time he has tried twice and failed."

Spook held himself alert for the slightest current of air that might blow him apart from the others, but none came. And still Jamie made no attempt to pick him out. "What is he going to *do*?" worried Spook.

He heard the Head Witch cry, "Two out of three — two out of three. Whoever wins this point gets the familiar." And the witches echoed, "Two out of three — two out of three."

Suddenly Jamie turned and walked a little distance away. Then he swung around, came hurtling back, and threw himself into the pile of leaves. He rolled over and over in them. Sitting up, he grabbed a great armful of them and threw it into the air. Autumn leaves came floating down all around him, in his hair, on his eyes, about his shoulders, and — in his lap — sat Spook, a solid little dog once more.

"That does it!" shrieked the Head Witch. "That gives the familiar to the boy."

"No, no!" cried Grimalda.

"Yes, yes," corrected the Head Witch. "Two points out of three. You heard the rules."

Jamie just sat on where he was and hugged Spook, who snuggled blissfully against him.

"You have lost the contest, Grimalda," said the Head Witch. "But you mustn't be downcast. There is a second prize."

She reached into her wide sleeves, her wrinkled lips smiling mysteriously. "And here it is!" she announced. Out of the deep, black folds she pulled a tiny black kitten.

"Take it," she said. "This is a *proper* familiar and, as it is only a young one, perhaps you will find a spell against sneezing to put on it before next Halloween."

Grimalda started to reply, but then her nose began to twitch and she clapped her hand over her face instead. Snatching up the little cat, which spat ill-naturedly at her, she hurried to her broom. They heard one last "Away" as the broom took flight and disappeared over the lonely hillside.

"And now," said the Head Witch. "And now —"
Jamie stood up with Spook beside him.

The Head Witch rose from her seat and moved
toward them — closer and still closer. Her eyes
flashed in their deep sockets, and two red flames
flared in them. A wind began to blow loud in
Spook's ears, his head reeled, and he blinked hard
to keep his eyes on hers. Darkness fell all about
them, blotting out the witches and their cave and
the light from the moon. Only the twin flames
from the Head Witch's eyes glowed on. But after
a while they flickered and slowly dwindled away.
Spook blinked again to find them in the distance,

and when he opened his eyes, the darkness was gone.

He was standing beside Jamie in the quiet kitchen they had left such a long time ago. The clock ticked on the shelf, and there was still a lingering smell of gingerbread on the air.

The kitchen door flew open and Mr. Brugle burst through, with the children crowding behind him.

"Jamie!" he cried.

"He's here!" sighed Evelina.

"Where's he been?" demanded John.

"He's got the little dog with him," said Susan.

Jamie took a step toward them.

"Yes," he said. "I have the little dog. And now he's mine. His name is Spook."

Spook thought of something he would like to say, but he remembered that they wouldn't understand him. And then he remembered something else. He looked quickly behind him. Just as he thought, his tail had begun to wag again. Slowly at first — and then faster, faster, faster. As though it would never stop.